This book belongs to: ....

Many thanks are due to Robbie Brennan and Dr. Phillip Smyly of the Maritime Museum of Ireland at Dun Laoire for their time and expertise and for providing access to Patrick Daly's model of the Asgard II. Thanks are also due to Simon Stevens and James Nurse at the National Maritime Museum at Greenwich, London, and Noreen Marshall at the Museum of Childhood at Bethnal Green, London.

Special thanks to Finola Goggin (Bosun), Sean McLaughlin and the offices and crew of Asgard II. Having sailed on the Asgard II in a force nine gale I can say she truly is a ship-shape ship! While I have used her as a model for the Colander, the resemblance is purely cosmetic.

May the Asgard sail on safely for many decades to come.

There are deliberate omissions and mistakes in the details of the ship in the pictures. These are to accommodate the story (if I had included all the ropes, for instance, the pictures would be covered in them!). All mistakes, deliberate or otherwise, are my own and certainly not due to lack of help from those mentioned above. Of course, if you find a *real* mistake, I shall claim artistic licence . . .

M-L.F.

For Roisín Law and her tale of a voyage . . . and for Ollie and Oisín, with love.

M-L.F.

First published in 2002 in Great Britain by Gullane Children's Books
This paperback edition published in 2006 by
Gullane Children's Books
an imprint of Pinwheel Limited,
Winchester House, 259-269 Old Marylebone Road,
London NW1 5XJ

1 3 5 7 9 10 8 6 4 2

Text and illustrations © Marie-Louise Fitzpatrick 2002

The right of Marie-Louise Fitzpatrick to be identified
as the author and illustrator of this work has been asserted by her
in accordance with the Copyright, Designs and Patents Act, 1988.

A CIP record for this title is available from the British Library.

ISBN-13: 978-1-86233-637-7
ISBN-10: 1-86233-637-7

Printed and bound in China

You, Me and the Big Blue Sea

Marie-Louise Fitzpatrick

GULLANE
CHILDREN'S BOOKS

When you were a baby we went to sea . . .

When you were a baby we went to sea, didn't we?
You, Aunt Alice and me, all three. And a big, big trunk.

But you were only a baby,
you wouldn't remember.

We waved bye-bye, didn't we? Then we were away, just like that, without any bother.

But you were only a baby, you wouldn't remember.

So off we sailed, didn't we?
There was nothing to see but the sea, the big blue sea.

But you were only a baby,
you wouldn't remember.

Then we heard a screeching
sound, didn't we?
But it was only a bird.
A pretty bird, up high in the sky.

But you were only a baby,
you wouldn't remember.

Then there were lots of
birdies, weren't there?
We fed them bags of bread.
Bags and bags.
You'd never think
they could eat so much.

But you were only a baby,
you wouldn't remember.

So we went for our afternoon nap, didn't we?
Down to our cabins and up in our bunks.
And there was nothing to see but the sea.

But you were only a baby,
you wouldn't remember.

We sat at the captain's table
for dinner, didn't we?
It was very nice.
But when we asked for jelly,
there wasn't any.
Now wasn't that funny?

But you were only a baby,
you wouldn't remember.

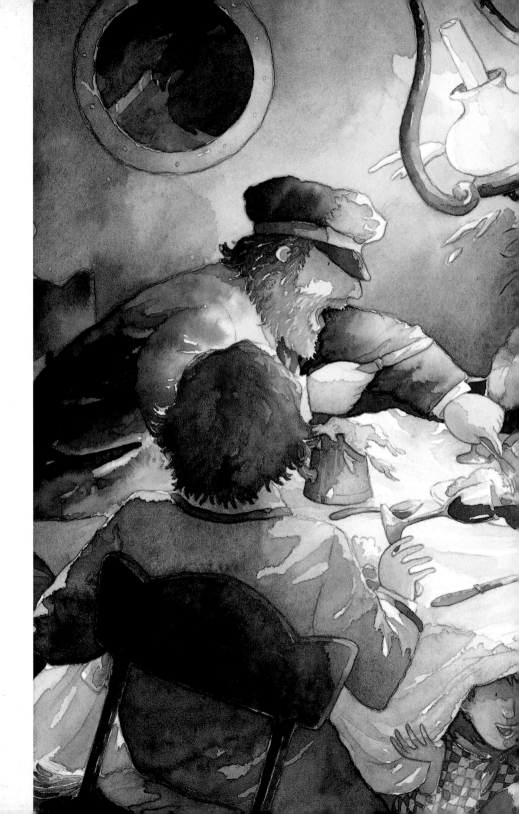

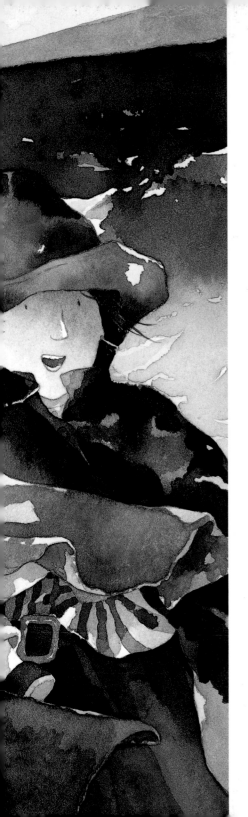

We went on deck for a little fresh air, didn't we?
The captain sailed such a ship-shape ship.
We knew we'd sleep snug that night,
down in our cabin and up in our bunks.

But you were only a baby, you wouldn't remember.

Next morning we woke, and there we were, weren't we?
Aunt Alice couldn't wait to get on to the pier.
But we were sad to leave that ship, you and me, weren't we?

But you were only a baby,
you wouldn't remember.

We were sad to leave,
weren't we?
Our feet were all wet,
but that didn't matter.
We were sad to leave
that little ship.
We went home on another
one, now why was that?

I don't remember, do you?

But of course you don't,
you were only a baby.

Other Gullane Children's Books
for you to enjoy

Izzy and Skunk

Marie-Louise Fitzpatrick

The Sorcerer's Apprentice

Sally Grindley • Thomas Taylor

I'm a Tiger Too!

Marie-Louise Fitzpatrick

Do You Still Love Me?

Charlotte Middleton